The Selfish Giant

Written by Oscar Wilde

Retold by Tanya Landman

Illustrated by Agata Krawczyk

Collins

Chapter 1

Every day after school, the children crept into the Giant's garden.
No one had told them they could. But then, no one had told
them they couldn't. They were doing no harm, they said to
each other. The Giant wasn't there. He'd been away for years
and years. None of them even knew what he looked like.

They climbed the trees and hid in the bushes. They played football and ran races over the lawns. And when they grew tired of all that, they lay in the long grass and listened to the birds singing.

Day after day, the children played in the garden. It was a wonderful, happy place until …

3

The Giant came back!

He'd been travelling for a long time and was feeling tired and cross.

He didn't want to see anybody. He didn't want to talk to anybody.

All he wanted to do was go to bed and sleep.

When he saw the children running around in his garden, he was angry.

"YOU'RE NOT ALLOWED IN HERE!" he shouted.

"GET OUT! GO AWAY! DON'T COME BACK!"

4

He chased them, yelling and shouting so loudly that leaves were ripped from the trees. The flowers hid their heads under the earth. The birds flew away.

He stood alone in the middle of the lawn. "IT'S MY GARDEN!" he roared. "MINE! MINE! MINE"

5

To stop the children ever coming back, he built a great big wall topped with broken glass and barbed wire. He put up signs.

KEEP OUT

STAY AWAY

PRIVATE

All summer long, the children had nowhere to play.

6

Chapter 2

Summer turned into autumn and then winter. Snow flew over the city, throwing great white flakes from the sky. Her brother Frost slid over ponds and puddles turning them to ice.

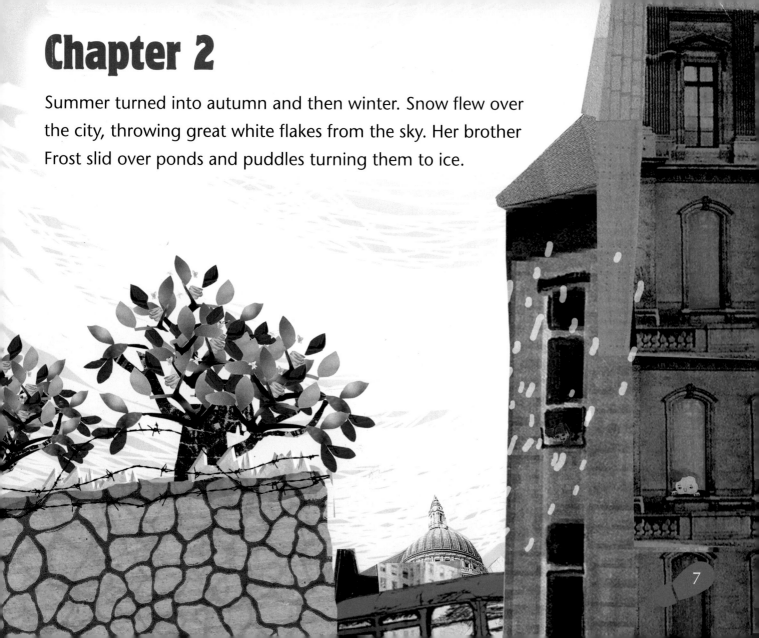

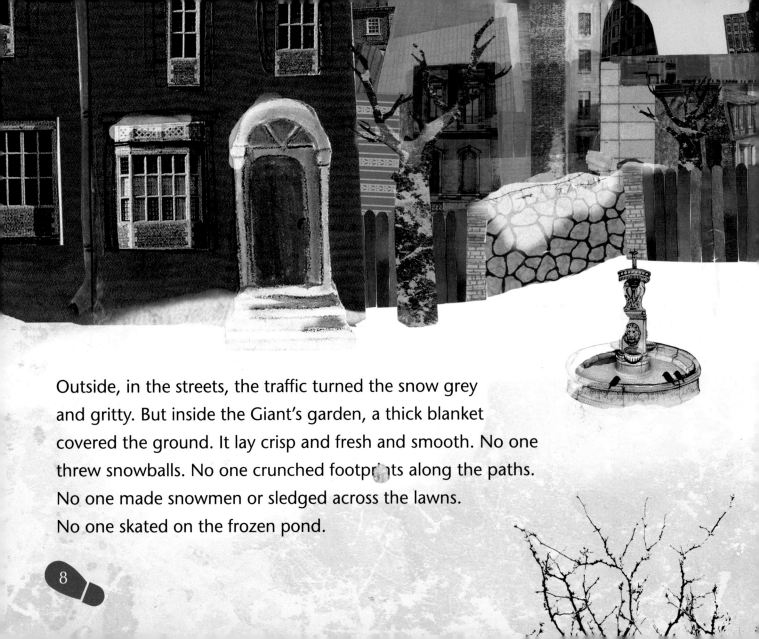

Outside, in the streets, the traffic turned the snow grey
and gritty. But inside the Giant's garden, a thick blanket
covered the ground. It lay crisp and fresh and smooth. No one
threw snowballs. No one crunched footprints along the paths.
No one made snowmen or sledged across the lawns.
No one skated on the frozen pond.

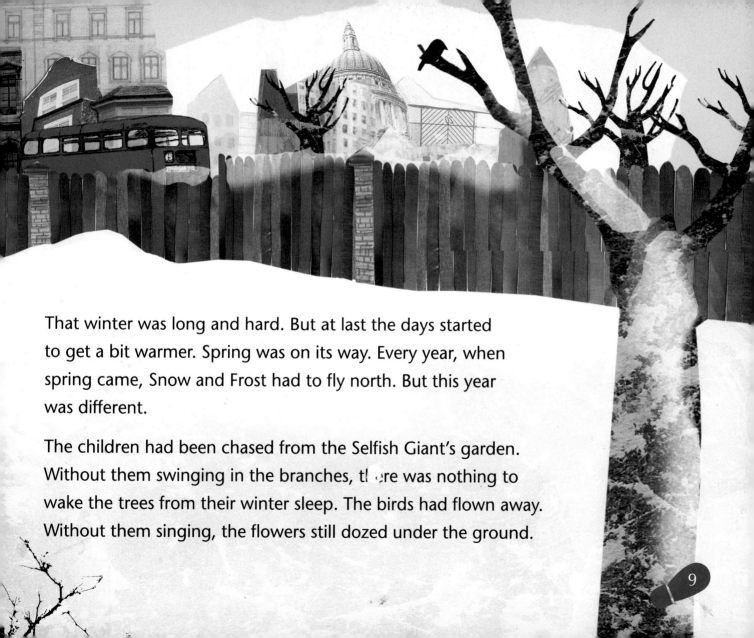

That winter was long and hard. But at last the days started
to get a bit warmer. Spring was on its way. Every year, when
spring came, Snow and Frost had to fly north. But this year
was different.

The children had been chased from the Selfish Giant's garden.
Without them swinging in the branches, there was nothing to
wake the trees from their winter sleep. The birds had flown away.
Without them singing, the flowers still dozed under the ground.

Snow and Frost were delighted. "We can stay here forever,"
Snow said to her brother. "This will be our home."

"We should celebrate," Frost replied. "In fact, let's have a party."

They invited Hail and North Wind.

The four friends began to dance. Snow whirled around
the Giant's house. North Wind screamed down his chimneys.
Frost breathed over the windows, and Hail drummed on the roof.

The Giant huddled down into his bed, waiting for the spring.
But it never came.

On the other side of the wall, the children watched spring turn to summer and then autumn. But in the garden nothing changed. No flowers turned to seed. No leaves changed their colours. No fruit hung from the trees. The snow and ice got deeper and thicker and the air got colder and colder.

Under his blankets, the Giant was miserable. "What's happened?" he said to himself. "Why is the spring so late?" He was all alone. There was no one to answer him.

Snow and Frost and Hail and North Wind danced more and more wildly.
They laughed and shrieked and made so much noise, the Giant put his
fingers in his ears. Day and night, he had no peace.

13

Chapter 3

But then one morning, the Giant woke with a shock.

It was quiet. Hail had stopped drumming on the roof. North Wind had stopped screaming down the chimneys. Frost had gone from the windows and Snow – where was Snow?

The silence was broken by the sound of sweet music. It was so long since the Giant had heard birdsong that for a moment he didn't know what it was.

Throwing off his blankets, he went to the window.

When he looked out, he saw the children had crept through
a hole in the wall. They'd climbed into trees, which had woken
up and burst into leaf. All around them birds were singing.
Snowdrops and daffodils had poked their heads above
the ground. It was a wonderful sight.

16

But in the furthest corner of the garden, it was still winter.
The Giant could see a boy standing underneath a tree. But he was
so small he couldn't climb it no matter how hard he tried. He was
crying as North Wind snapped around his ankles and Hail threw
stones at his head.

Pity melted the Giant's selfish heart. He tiptoed downstairs and opened the door. When the other children saw him, they ran away, and the whole garden became winter again. Snow whirled in a great blizzard across the grass. Frost snapped off the flowers' heads and turned the pond to ice.

The little boy didn't run away. His eyes were so full of tears,
he didn't even see the Giant coming. Gently, the Giant picked
him up and lifted him onto a branch. And at once the tree
covered itself in blossom.

The Giant looked at the boy. It was strange, he thought. The boy was so small. So young. He could only be two or three. And yet his eyes seemed as old as the stars.

The boy didn't say a word, but sat gazing at the Giant. His eyes – that were as deep and dark as the endless universe – glowed with sorrow and sadness and joy and love.

When the other children saw the boy smiling at the Giant, they came running back. The spring came with them.

Turning away from the boy, the Giant went to work. He fetched a hammer and knocked down the wall. "It's your garden now," he told the children. "Play wherever you like. Make yourselves at home."

They climbed the trees and hid in the bushes. They played football and ran races over the lawns. And when they grew tired, they lay in the long grass and listened to the birds singing.

22

The Giant sat in the warm sunshine and watched them. But he couldn't
see the little boy he'd lifted into the tree. And when he asked,
"Where is he?" the children said they didn't know. They'd never seen
him before. They didn't know who he was or where he lived.

After that, the children played in the Giant's garden every day. But the young boy with eyes as old as stars never came again. The Giant often wondered about him. Who was he? Where had he come from?
Where had he gone? The Giant missed him.

Chapter 4

The seasons changed. Years went by. The children grew up and had children of their own who played in the garden every day after school. The Giant got older and weaker, but he still loved to sit and watch them. He loved the plants and flowers, but he loved seeing the children run and climb most of all.

And then – one winter's morning when he'd grown very old and frail –
the Giant looked out of his window. In the furthest corner was a tree
he'd never seen before. Its golden branches bore silver fruit and white
blossom, but the Giant hardly noticed because – standing underneath
it – was the young boy! He'd grown no taller or older than the last
time the Giant had seen him.

The Giant's legs were stiff and his joints ached. It took him a long
time to make his way down the stairs and into the garden.
As the Giant hobbled across the lawns towards him, the young boy
with eyes as old as stars smiled.

"You let me play once in your garden," he said. "Today you shall come with me to mine."

He held out his hand, and the Giant took it. And all at once his aches and pains vanished.

When the children ran into the garden that afternoon, the Giant was nowhere to be seen.

There was only a tree all covered with dazzling white blossom, whose golden branches hung heavy with silver fruit.